Who Is the Boss?

Josse Goffin

Clarion Books

New York

I am the boss!

No. I am the boss!

I am taller than you.

But I am more terrifying.

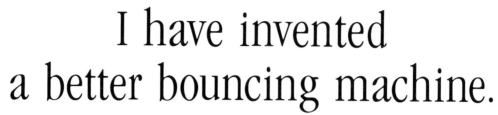

I have invented a better bouncing machine.

My invention is supremely superior.

My manners are finer than yours.

But I am a much nicer person.

I am master of the sword.

And I am king of all that I see.

The moon is my special friend.

But you can't spin like a top!

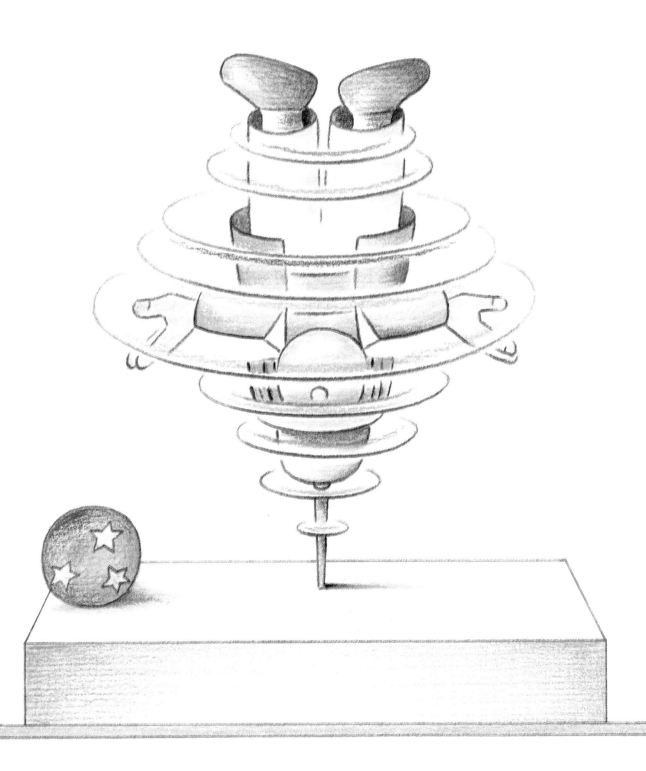

No weight is too heavy for me.

My balance is perfect.

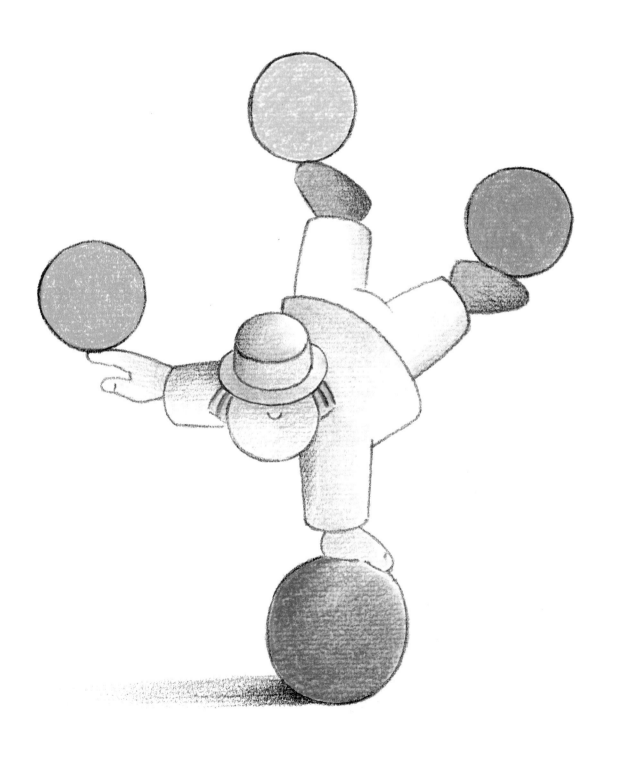

Even lightning obeys my command.

I am exceptionally gifted.

No one bugles better than I.

And no one moves faster than I.

I am the boss!
No! I am!

CRAACK!

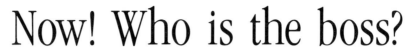

Now! Who is the boss?

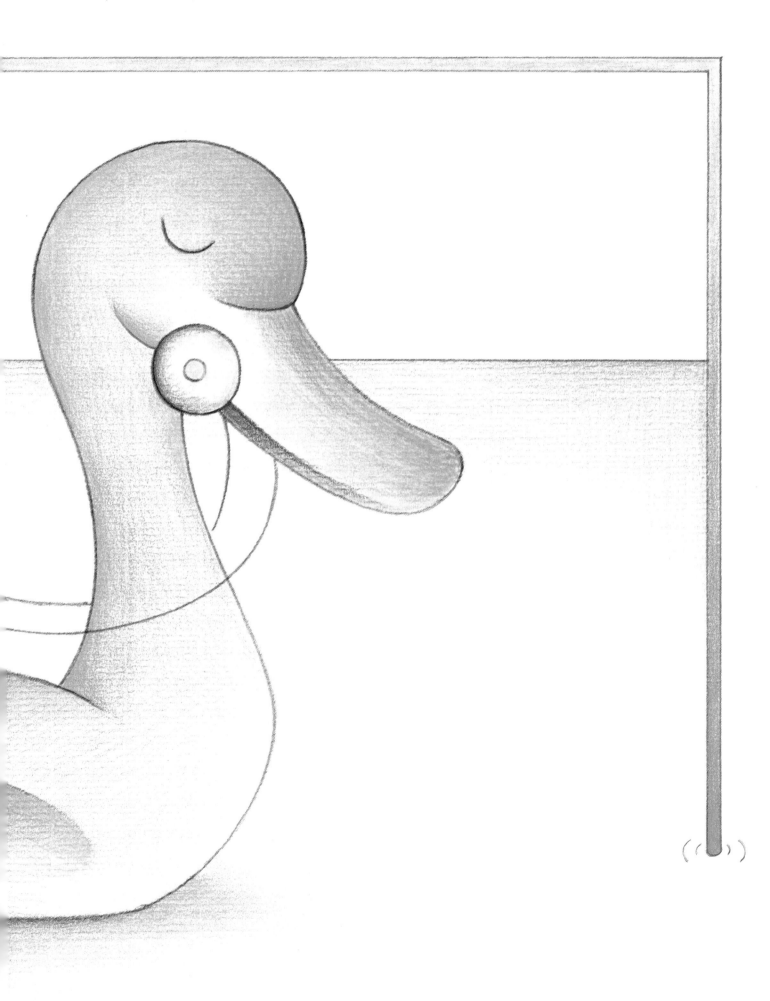

Clarion Books
a Houghton Mifflin Company imprint
215 Park Avenue South, New York, NY 10003

Production and © 1992 Rainbow Grafics Intl-Baronian Books SC, Brussels, Belgium
Rue de la Vallée 32, B-1050 Brussels, Belgium.

For information about permission to reproduce selections from
this book, write to Permissions, Houghton Mifflin Company,
2 Park Street, Boston, MA 02108.

Printed in Belgium.

Library of Congress Cataloging-in-Publication Data

Goffin, Josse.
[C'est qui le chef?   English]
Who is the boss? / by Josse Goffin.
p.   cm.
Translation of: C'est qui le chef?
Summary: Two power-hungry passengers learn who's really
in charge when their boat sinks after each tries to outdo the
other with preposterous feats.
ISBN 0-395-61192-X
[1. Leadership—Fiction.   2. Humorous stories.]   I. Title.
PZ7.G55697Wh   1992
[E]—dc20   91-23989
                                                CIP
                                                AC

10 9 8 7 6 5 4 3 2 1